The WET DRY Book

By Kate Spohn

Random House 🏠 New York

Copyright © 2002 by Kate Spohn. All rights reserved under International and Pan-American Copyright Conventions. Published in the United States of America by Random House, Inc., New York, and simultaneously in Canada by Random House of Canada Ltd., Toronto. ISBN: 0-375-82186-4 Library of Congress Control Number: 2001093774 www.randomhouse.com/kids Printed in China First Edition August 2002 10 9 8 7 6 5 4 3 2 1 RANDOM HOUSE and colophon are registered trademarks of Random House, Inc.

I like books.
I like tea.
I like the *purr, purr*
of Kitten and me.

I like sweaters.
I like home.
I like the ring, ring
of the telephone.

I like Turtle.

I like Guppy.

I like the **splash, splash** of my puppy.

I like umbrellas.
I like coats.
I like the **plink, plink**
of musical notes.

I like bunnies.
I like bears.

I like the

creak,

creak

of the stairs.

I like ducks.
I like brown.
I like the
gurgle,
gurgle
of a river
running down.

I like boats.
I like fish.
I like the slurp, slurp
of a kiss.

I like shadows.
I like lace.
I like the crackle,
crackle
of the fireplace.

I like bubbles.
I like mice.
I like the *whisper, whisper*
of something nice.

I like clouds.
I like rain.
I like the **CLACKETY, CLACKETY**
of a train.

I like pj's.
I like socks.
I like the **tick, tick**
of my clocks.

I like bed.
I like pie.
I like the *hello, hello*
after good-bye.

I like mud.
I like snails.
I like the **plop, plop**
of water in pails.

I like worms.
I like bugs.
I like the **glub,
glub**
of wet-on-wet hugs.

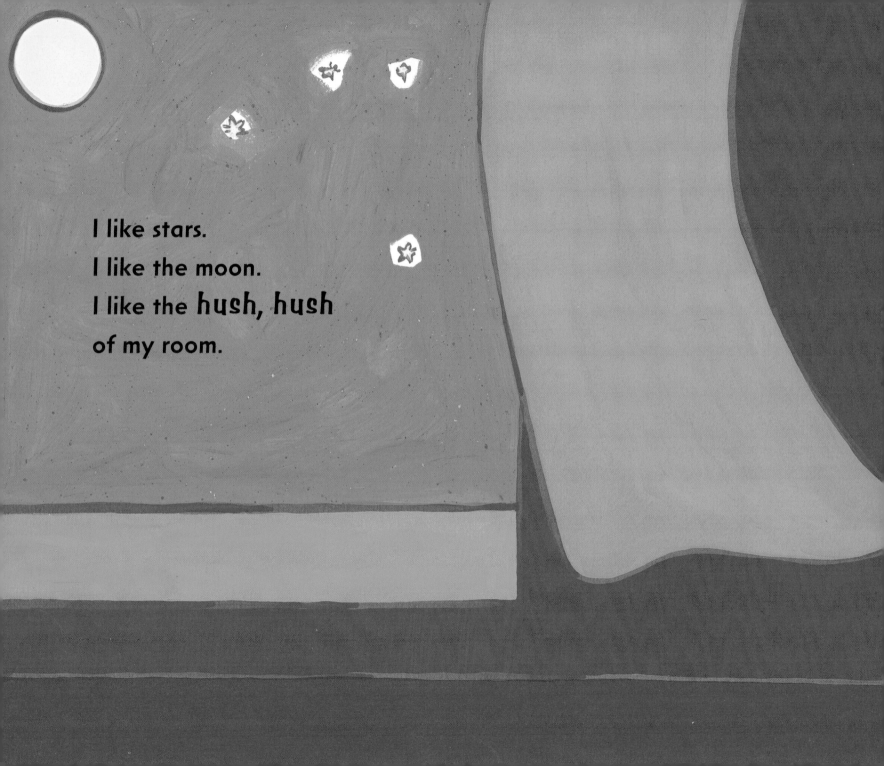

I like stars.
I like the moon.
I like the hush, hush
of my room.

I like thunder.
I like light.
I like the
**bang,
bang**
of the night!